Power Exchange
Books

First Edition

Published by The Nazca Plains Corporation
Las Vegas, Nevada
2008

ISBN: 978-1-934625-74-3

Published by

The Nazca Plains Corporation ®
4640 Paradise Rd, Suite 141
Las Vegas NV 89109-8000

Cover, Lancera
Art Director, Blake Stephens

Power Exchange
Books

First Edition

Issue Coordinator, slave lara
Series Editor, Robert Rubel, PhD

Foreword

By Bob Rubel

I'm particularly proud of slave lara for the tremendous amount of time, trouble, and work that she put into this issue of *Power Exchange Books' Resource Series*. This has truly been a labor of love.

This book, has been compiled by slave lara, who is the owner of the Consortium bearing the same name. Here, you will read a delightful cross-section of thoughts about slavery written by members of her Consortium. In my opinion, this book is a fun and interesting read. I hope you enjoy it as much as I have.

This series of books, this *Resource Series*, is intended for the entire kink community in all its forms. This series of books is intended to give voice to people who make up the myriad specialty subcultures and fetishes in this world. In the back of this book, I've listed a wide range of topics that are currently being considered. If you are interested in contributing to these topics (until that book comes out) please contact me.

I've thoroughly enjoyed meeting people at kink conferences and seeing how excited they get about contributing to this project. By the way, while these books are not going to big sellers, all royalties are going to a combination of Leather resources, including:

- Leather Archives and Museum (LA&M)
- Leather Leadership Conference (LLC)
- Masters and slaves Together (MAsT)
- National Coalition for Sexual Freedom (NCSF)
- Woodhull Foundation

In Leather Heart and Spirit,

Bob Rubel (Dr. Bob)
Series Editor

Contents

10/2008
Sammi,
I hope you enjoy this compilation of essays. Thank you for being a great new friend.
Hugs,
Slave lara

Preface

From the Coordinator of this Issue

Art of slavery

By slave lara

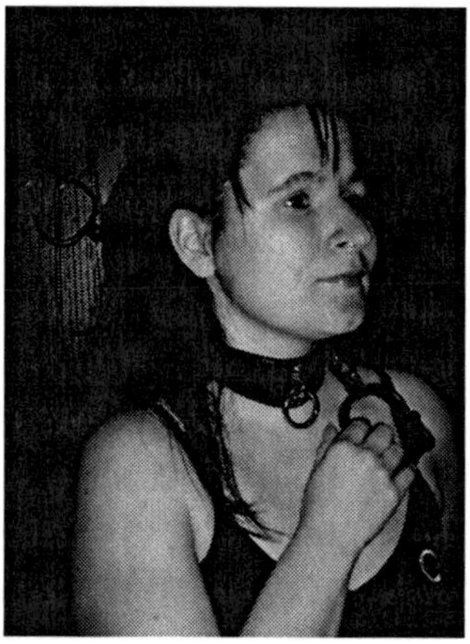

Leather

Honor. Integrity. Respect. Loyalty. Beauty.

slavery

Honor. Integrity. Respect. Loyalty. Trust. Communication. Dignity.

Transparency. Obedience. Service. Beauty.

Art

Expressive. Skill. Mastery. Stimulating of senses. Creativity. Imagination. Curiosity. Focused. Tranquil. Beauty

My Art is slavery. My slavery is Leather. Leather is my Art of slavery.

My Art of slavery is Beautiful and Tranquil.

I welcome you all to the Art of slavery edition of the Power Exchange Magazine. For me personally, the terminology of "art of slavery" is very near and dear to me and is a phrase that I coined in my own creed as a slave many years ago. I am honored that this edition is taking a moment to honor the world of what I see within my eyes as pure beauty.

I have been often asked "How can there be an "art" to slavery" when slavery is stigmatically about "obedience"? For me, one must transcend past the stigmatic mindset; and rather in my opinion, slavery is in the depths and core of me and encompasses much more to me than just obedience. The art of slavery is a passionate song that is being written in my life and is a song that is being composed via the Power Exchange between my owner and me. When all of the beginning aforementioned adjectives are put into effect into one's own slavery or Power Exchange, the transcendence becomes a powerful work of art within one's life and relationship.

Within this edition of the Power Exchange series, I am proud to bring you a collection of essays of many different long term members of a consortium that I founded in 2005 entitled, Art of slavery (Aos). Our members come from all walks of life and many different diverse experiences and relationships. All of these writers are real life slaves living the day to day realities of what slavery is truly about. They are not famous. They are not speakers, although some may be. Many are not even teachers; although yet again, some may be. Each bring with them a wonderfully beautiful perspective based on their own experiences. They are highly passionate, and these particular writers are truly living the beauty and the art of what slavery is about. They are normally those individuals that you see behind the scenes in a very quiet humble way planning munches, events, gatherings, parties, etc. They are the tireless volunteers that never ask for anything other than the wonderful opportunity of providing a service to make people happy. Many are what could be perceived as workhorses. Some are happiest when being solely at their Owner's feet. Others are perceived as not even being slaves at all, but rather very strong type A personalities that get the job done. These type A individuals often are questioned on if they are dominant and/ or slave when in reality they bow their heads and souls to one – their owner - in the most beautiful tranquil way in private. These writers are the reality.

When I first started Aos, I personally found there to be a void of information related to the slave mindset. I found myself personally lost in a sea yearning for more information on slavery and/or wanting to bond with another slave like myself. I found myself tired of reading of the fantasy and non reality views of slavery. I also found that within my local community, I was standing out as an odd bird that had this unusual mindset that some could have perceived and construed as edgy as my mindset was not based on play alone. My mindset rather evolved around the power exchange, obedience, transparency, communication, relinquishing of my entire being - mind, body, heart, soul, and spirit. To many, these ideals seemed foreign, unique, obscure, edgy, abusive, and on the tier of being a doormat. To me, I found great fulfillment in providing service in the most beautiful ways possible. It wasn't until I met my current owner, Lord Brick, that I learned what Power Exchange truly is. It was not about me. It was not about him. It was about us and the song that we, he, and I created within our own power exchange based on his desires and our compatibility in that respect.

In the essays to come, you will see that I am not alone. After the starting of the Aos group, I found rapidly that there were many more slaves with this same beauty within them. We all have our own diverse beautiful ways in which we all serve our owners. We all have our own diverse beautiful ways in which we relinquish. We all have our own diverse beautiful ways in which we surrender our mind, body, heart, spirit and soul. What we do all have in common though is that we all are slaves and share the same tranquil spirit and emotions that our forms of slavery provide as diverse as we may seem on the surface.

On this blustery Christmas evening here in Pennsylvania, as I sit here reflecting on this essay, the song, "The Rose" is playing in the background for inspiration while I type. If you have never heard this song before, I would very much encourage you to take a moment to listen to it in your own relationship. As much as the word "Love" is one of the age old debates within this Master/slave (M/s) lifestyle, for me this song has a very subtle element that is a lovely reminder to me of the epitome of what my M/s relationship is about. It is about surrendering and relinquishing all of one's self. I am the rose and my owner is the seed to me blooming and relinquishing. It is truly an endless aching need, yearning and hunger that a slave feels to their core to be in service and to be a slave. Without the owner nurturing the seed, the water, the caring, and the tending of their slave, the power exchange is not complete. When one sits back and really looks at this dynamic, one cannot dispute how artistic this all seems.

I very much have a strong musical background as a piano player and composer. A few months back, a good Aos friend of mine and writer, Evy, requested from my owner permission to write an article about myself and the Art of slavery group. One of the most difficult questions for me to answer that she posed at the time was – "What does art of slavery mean to you?" When I sat back and really thought about it, my slavery truly reminded me of the never ending amounts of songs that I have composed. In this instance, the life that I lead is the song that is being written by the seed of my owner. I firmly believe that if you asked any slave in this lifestyle the same question, a very similar yet diverse response would surface.

To continue that thought, a few days back I posed to the Art of slavery members, "How have you been touched by a Master's Hand?" What sparked that question was that I had just finished reading the poem and watching the 18 minute movie "Touch of a Master's Hand". This poem has always been one of the most powerful poems that has fed my slavery over the years. In reading, it causes me to reflect that as much as I am like a sweet violin that has been dusty here and there over the years, I am ever touched by a Master's Hand. My favorite quote from the poem reinforces this by saying, "But the Master comes. And the foolish crowd never can quite understand. The worth of a soul and the change that is wrought by the Touch of a Master's Hand.". This quote reminds me of the time where I was searching for a void of information and I always seemed to be misunderstood by those that didn't understand the impact of a Master's Hand and the impact due to the depth of a Power Exchange. This impact to me is my song, my art, my slavery, and ultimately my Leather within this Lifestyle.

If I ever had anything to say regarding the Art of slavery, it would truly be about the realm of the impact of both transcending in one's self, one's relationship, one's slavery as well as taking faith in the impact of a Master's Hand upon a Power Exchange.

In closing, I encourage each one of you that read this particular edition, to truly take the time to absorb what each of these slaves are speaking about and see the beauty and the art behind each of their words. The ways by which each of these slaves have been touched by a Master, Mistress and/or Dominant throughout the course of their lives speaks volumes about the people that they are today - with beautiful spirits. As much as they all have been "touched", they all bring an internal spirit and flame that can never be quenched no matter what life brings to each of them. Each has an internal flame that will continue to shine throughout the course of their lives as they strive for their total purpose - to surrender completely.

I shared at the beginning of this essay what adjectives describe my Art of slavery.

I ask in return of all of you -

What is your Leather? What is your creed?

What is your slavery? What is your Mastery?

What is your song?

Mine is being owned completely and touched.

Mind - Body - Heart - Spirit - Soul

That is Art of slavery.

Resources:

Master's Hand:

> http://www.atthewell.com/touch/index.php

The Rose:

> http://www.amcbroom.com/rose.html

Art of slavery:

> http://groups.yahoo.com/group/Artofslavery

About the Author:

slave lara is from Philadelphia, PA, and is a 34 year old, bisexual, polyamorous slave and mentor that enjoys extremely intense sensations. She is owned and collared to Lord Brick as his little girl and kitten in an ever growing total power exchange (TPE) M/s dynamic. slave lara is the Founder and Moderator of the real-time and online group entitled, Art of slavery (Aos); as well as, is the Assistant Director of the MAsT: Philadelphia chapter and one of the primary event planners for M/s related functions in her region including the creation and coordination of the Northeast "M/s Extravaganza" event. Additionally, she co-presents a slave time management class; as well as, presents on Transparency, Communication, Intimacy and Mentoring as part of the "slave track" program for both the Northeast M/s Conference and the Southwest Leather Conference. Aos is slave lara's heart and soul which was created in 2005 in an effort to fill a void in the national slavery community. Aos is a group that provides and encourages real life concrete information, support, networking and inspiration to those of the slave mindset in a safe haven. slave lara is widely known for her viewpoints on transparency, communication, diversity, mentoring, protocols and rituals as she is often seen as a Higher Protocol slave. In conjunction as part of her own personal mission as a slave, she provides constant every day support in the Northeast Region of the United States (PA, NJ, DE, VA, NY, MD) to new submissives entering the lifestyle and performs a lot of mentoring associated with that.

The Master's Touch

By slave tanarria

She sleeps, resting in the darkness,
her heart cold and worn.
To her, life is done.
No one to be trusted, no one to be loved.
Her weary eyes look around....watching...wondering
if there would ever be a time of sweet love.
She shakes her head and slowly returns to sleep,
sighing softly as she still somehow hopes,
tossing and turning in the night.
She sits night after night, day after day,
learning of that which she craves.
Her body yearning for that which she sees,
that which brings her soul alive.
Her words dance on the screen,
taking her away to another world.
A place where Men are Masters
and women are slaves.

PEBRS

Her heart flutters with life,
yet still wistful, her body aches.
The Master comes stealthily in the night,
slowly unbinding her heart strand by strand,
warming it slowly, holding it in the palm of His hand.
He guides her spirit with a firm hand, her heart with a sweet
caress
His powerful arms draw her to Him, holding her close
as she fights her way to the surface once again.
He holds out His hand and her heart is captured by His,
as she places her spirit, her life and her body at His feet.
She lifts her hand to His and entrusts it to His care,
All bindings are gone, her soul awakens and lives.

Growing in Slavery - He IS Master, and I am slave

By slave bethie

Here I am again, Thursday night, stressed from working out of town. Beeping and creeping my way through rainy weather and rush hour traffic around the Baltimore beltway. I feel frantic, the red tail lights in front of me stretch endlessly and all I want... no, need... is to be in the most secure place I know, at my Master's feet. I call to give my best estimate for an arrival time, and know he feels my anxiety from my quivering voice.

Monday through Thursday like clockwork I put on my professional image, both inside and out, and plunge into my weekly world - fast paced, high stress, deadline driven by clients with oftentimes unrealistic expectations. I am in a career I love. I thrill in the challenge of an ever changing industry, of the complexity of technology and designing solutions; but, by the end of the week, I needed to be brought back to where I belong.

The wipers beat a relentless rhythm as I leave the miles behind me, and I finally cross into my home state. Mentally, I began to prepare myself. It is time to leave the "professional me" behind, and find my way back to my inner self.

As I pull into the driveway, the candlelight glows dimly in the window. Slipping into the house, I silently make my way to deposit groceries in the kitchen, then on to the bedroom to leave my suitcase. I look up, feeling my soul reach for the beginnings of release. I lift the pink and black leather collar from the hook on the bedroom wall. Slipping off my shoes, I pad softly to the living room where he sits waiting. The hushed music starts to filter through my mind as I pull my focus inward. I kneel wordlessly, shoulders back, knees parted, straight, and proud. I place the collar on the floor at his feet. My hands, palms up, then rest on my thighs, in a classic Gorean slave nadu position. I close my eyes as the words of my litany began to flow from my mind to my heart to my soul. Anytime I have been out of the house for any length of time – it is the same. The protocol, the tradition, helps pull me back to where my soul always knew it belonged. "He is Master, and I am slave. He is Owner, and I am owned. He is to command, and I am to obey. His is to be pleased, and I am to please. Why is this? Because he is Master, and I am slave."

I feel his eyes on me, but I dare not move, nor speak. My heart rate slows, my breathing evens, and my body relaxes as I hold my position. Again, the mantra starts in my mind. At last, I hear the creak of his leather chair. His hand lightly touches my hair, stroking it lovingly, and his fingers caress my face. Finally his hand comes into my line of vision, and I lean forward, kissing it, then clinging to it and kissing it more fervently. I lower my head, lifting my hair from the nape of my neck. I can feel the strength of his fingers as he buckles the leather collar over my silver, permanent one. I am home, no longer in charge, no longer the decision maker, leader, and the problem solver. I am - his slave.

This protocol and others didn't just happen; and, it wasn't just something he arbitrarily decided. A simple collaring and an opportunity to center myself, create the transition I need. As a professional consultant; tossed about by clients all week, I would return home near frantic. I was filled with stress, ready to rant about who did what, and why.

Early in our relationship, my outburst and rantings began the minute I walked through the door. I would see his face set, his jaw clench, and my mind would scream, "You need to stop talking now!", but it was like a barking dog. Once he starts barking, and keeps going, it gets more and more insistent and annoying. I distinctively remember the day he stood, and simply said, "STOP!"

He walked to me, pushing me down to my knees and said, "Shhhh, do not say ONE more word. From now on, when you enter the home, you will put your things away - without talking! You will find me, come and kneel at my side, and focus yourself inward. Find your soul; find your place as the slave you know you are. Then "I" will decide when you are settled, calmed, focused, and in the right head space." A very small part of me felt indignant. But I suppressed that initial response, knowing he was right. Now my home comings are peaceful and fulfilling. It wasn't always easy.

I remember the day I came in, knelt, and saw him cross the room to stand in front of me. As I kept my eyes lowered, finding my mind focused on the fact that his shoes were dirty, I waited. I fully expected his hand to appear in my line of vision, but it didn't. Instead he turned, moving through the bedroom into the bathroom. The sound of the shower startled me. Immediately my mind thought, "How dare you! I'm here kneeling. You aren't going to instantly acknowledge me???" I was truly flabbergasted. My mind was running a thousand directions at once. I COULD get up and just walk around! I COULD slip back out, and he would never hear me. I COULD talk out loud and while he was in the shower he would never know.

Then my spirit quickened, and my mind began to slip into focus. Yes, I COULD do any of those things, but we both knew I wouldn't. I started reciting in my head, forcing myself to think about each word, not just what the words meant, but what they meant to ME, and I calmed.

He was right. Once again, he read me better than I read myself. So often that is the case. He knew I was not settled when I came in. He knew I needed that longer time to focus, to calm, and to be alone with myself. When he finally returned, I knew I was ready. As always, I felt the world drop away, and my focus come back to where it belonged. His slave. His consensual slave. A place I had longed for as long as I can remember. A place I fantasized about, dreamed about, but never knew could really happen.

It's been just over four years since we met. We both had been looking for many years for the partner who understood, who shared the vision, and who longed for this depth in a relationship. It was difficult in the early days in learning about each other, our needs, desires, and wants, and learning to separate needs from wants. I was learning to let go of "the ways of the world", the molded person society tried to force me to become.

As a child, I had longed for a strong authority in my life. My mother was a true disciplinarian. I didn't find that a problem, although my sister rebelled against such firm control. She couldn't understand my submission to the authority anymore than I could understand her desire to thwart that authority at every turn.

At the age of 13, I vividly recall coming into the room where my elder sister and mother were chatting. They were discussing the type of men they were drawn to. In the depths of my being, I truly believed that all females felt as I did, that NEED to submit. So I spoke up. I tried to voice my urges, my needs for a "strong man, one who would set the rules, one who knew how things should be done, and one who would teach me." Words can't describe my horror when they both burst into laughter. It was the late '60s. "This is the time of women's lib, don't EVER talk like that. You will never get ahead in life wanting to be submissive to some man. Grow up," my mother admonished. I ran to my room, sobbing, and threw myself on my bed. How could I be so different? How can they not feel what I felt? How can I change what has always been inside me?

I spent years – through high school, college, graduate school – suppressing those needs. I had vowed to never share them again. I endured 10 years of a vanilla marriage, married to a man who simply could not take his place as the head of the home. I was constantly forced to become the decision maker, and the financial manager. I felt resentment start. It grew, until I finally had no respect left for him. He felt it too, and as things went from bad to worse, we ended it.

Through a series of experiences and meeting people unexpectedly, I was startled to find there were others who felt as I did. Not only were there others, they welcomed me. It was like finding the family I had never known. I made my share of mistakes along the way. But 4+ years ago when I met my Master, I knew I was where I belonged. We have built a life where he IS Master, and I AM his slave. My deepest joy comes from serving him. Yes, I serve him sexually, but it is so much more than that. His dominance is over the whole of me, not just my sexuality. I serve him in the way I keep our home, and in handing the "details" of everyday life.

In the past two years, I have done a great deal of soul searching about this Master/slave relationship. I believe anyone can blindly follow rules and orders that are barked

23

out by another person. We do it at work every day, but I have found a new level of peace and contentment in watching him, studying him, and learning to anticipate his needs, rather than waiting for him to have to give an order.

My time at home goes all too quickly. I find its Monday morning, and he helps me load the car. Before I leave he pulls in into his lap, cuddling me there as he rocks me in his big leather recliner.

"Who do you belong to, bethie?"

"I belong to you, Master."

"Who owns you?"

"You do, Master."

"And who loves you, and will be waiting for your return this week?"

"You do, Master."

He walks me to the car and waves as he stands in the driveway until I am out of sight.

The week starts; but, as the stress comes, my fingers slip to the sterling silver collar that is locked around my neck. My fingers play with the slave ring that is always on my finger. I feel his strength, his control, and my soul settles.

I know I can and will successfully face another week in my professional world.

How do I know?

Because he is Master, and I am slave.

About the Author:

bethie is the permanently collared and owned slave to Denny James (Daddy Denny). They have been together for 5 years, the past three years in a full time M/s relationship. They currently share a home in south central PA which they are working to turn into a lifestyle friendly B&B. Their relationship also includes the Age Play dynamic found within the BDSM community. Denny is her Daddy, she is his baby girl. She is 100% slave; yet at the same time, 100% his baby girl. They have been presenters and educators, sharing this part of their dynamic with others who are intrigued, interested, and curious about this unique dynamic. The BDSM community has known her as an active presenter, educator, group leader and mentor for almost 10 years. bethie runs a successful "munch group" in the south central PA area named Alternative Expressions. She took over this group when it had dwindled down to 4 attendees each month, and has helped it grow to more than 200 members with 30 to 40 "regulars" who now attend monthly. She is in the process of re-establishing monthly demos, education sessions and other events for the group. Her experiences, both positive and negative, have enabled her to be a positive asset and mentor to "new" people within the BDSM community. bethie is an intelligent, professional female, degreed in Mathematics. She works as a computer consultant for major clients along the east coast. When at home, bethie is fully in service to her Master, including running of the home domestically, handling finances, and taking responsibility for maintaining logs of visitors so as to know their preferences for future visits. She takes great pride in running a well maintained, efficient, and peaceful home for her Master, working to always make it his oasis.

A Slave of Strength

By slave tanarria

I am a woman of passion. I write about the type of passion that brings our emotions to the forefront when we hear of someone abusing children. I write about the type of passion that makes us angry when we hear of certain injustices in the world. I talk about the passion that brings my voice to crescendo and my fingers to type faster and faster without regard for the feelings of others. I talk about the passion of a woman who believes strongly in many things and believes there is right and wrong. My world has many such beliefs and I am passionate about each of them. I am a woman of truth, deep faith, and a strong moral belief system.

I am naturally submissive to certain personalities; however, I am a very strong woman and it takes a very special and strong dominant to take me there. I am a strong woman to most, submissive to few, and slave to one. I believe that a woman can be strong, demanding, and assertive; yet, yearn to submit with all she has to the right man that wins her trust and respect. I believe that it takes longer than a few days, weeks, or sometimes months to win that trust. Sometimes trust is never earned. As my lifestyle sister, slave lara stated in her introduction:

> "Others are perceived as not even being slaves at all, but rather very strong type A personalities that get the job done. These type A individuals often are questioned on if they are dominant and/or slave when in reality they bow their heads and souls to one – their owner - in the most beautiful tranquil way in private."

I, like many others, saw controlling, assertive personalities in slavery as a negative thing. I don't fit, I'm not "slave-like", and I'm not what people would call a "natural" slave or submissive; yet, I *am* a slave. If Master were asked, he would have no problem defending my position as a slave - *his* slave. Those that take the time to know me and the Master I serve would agree also.

I am driven to serve. I am driven to perfection. I am driven to take any demand made of me, meet the challenge, and then ask for more. I am constantly seeking to better myself and care for others' needs. The one thing I cannot do is change who I am. Words like graceful, quiet, calm, and serene do not fit me. When asked to jump, I jump first, and then ask how high on the way up. It is how I am wired, how I am made, and how I will always be. This does not mean I am not able to make changes or be trained in the ways that are most pleasing to the one I am with; after all, I *am* submissive and serve to please.

When my submissive or slave mindset is triggered, I become inwardly contemplative and quiet as I await my next command. I do not want to make decisions or think outside of what my one requires of me. Loud environments and casual conversation become almost an impossibility as I sink into a place in my heart where I am happiest. I crave the feeling of ownership, the collar and cuffs. I easily kneel and worship the feet of the one that cares for me and knows what to do with my slavery.

Now that I have explained who I am, I would like to clarify how this relates to my service and submission. My personality does not come without its challenges when my assertive controlling personality is drawn into a Master/slave relationship. My accepting and relinquishment of all power to the man I call Master has been a long and challenging road. There are more times than I care to admit that I must battle the controlling side and submit my will to Master, even though my very being is screaming, "NO!" One such instance challenged our relationship to its very core. Master asked me to submit my trust to him regarding a particularly divisive situation, and I desperately wanted to; however, my strong, controlling side was screaming out to be heard. I was waging an internal battle between needing to be heard, wanting to submit, and desperately wanting to surrender all to the man I had grown to love and trust with everything I had. To accomplish full surrender in a healthy and long term Master/slave relationship, I have had to ask myself the question, "What are my goals in a Master/slave relationship?"

My goals are to be pleasing, to submit and surrender all, to relinquish my power and control, to fight my natural instincts to be in charge, and to serve the one that has mastered me. My goals are clear because I love him, because he has earned my respect, and because I wish to please him and give him anything he desires. The next question I had to ask myself was, "What does it mean to be pleasing?"

To be pleasing means to work each day to discover the

things that please Master most. It may be washing and ironing his clothes, cleaning his toilet, or giving him an extravagant massage as my own body is exhausted from a long day at work, school, and completing homework. It may mean taking needles into my flesh or accepting a caning or flogging for his sadistic pleasure. It may mean sitting at his feet, processing his bills, or keeping his home comfortable and inviting. It means using my gifts for organization and planning to create a worry-free environment for him. He only needs to make his desires known and there is no question that it will be done, without micromanagement. Without a doubt, the perfect match of my personality and Master's needs work well together to create the exact environment he desires. Pleasing him brings me the greatest fulfillment I've ever known. However, I must remind myself that it is not exclusively about pleasing him. It is also about relinquishing power and control.

To relinquish power and control means first to recognize when my personality is working to overtake my true heart's desire – To submit and surrender. It's not always easy to recognize when I am missing the cues and feel the need for control escalating. In the past, stressful situations demanded I step up and take control of the situation. I am a problem solver and a perfectionist. My 17-year marriage, where I was head of the household; and, later living the life of a single mom, taught me how to take control of life's ups and downs. I had no choice. I am a survivor, and I have a passion for life. I purchased my first home, raised my daughter, worked full-time at a low paying position, and a second part-time job from home so I was still around to raise my daughter. I learned to do without, and to do whatever it takes to have the things I need to survive. All these things taught me how to take control of myself and my life, and I didn't need anyone's help. After all, it was my life.

When I first divorced, Master came into my life. Slowly, he gained my trust and it built my desire to relinquish and surrender all to him. However, he recognized my strengths and allowed me to come to him on my terms. Slowly, over many years, I have been able to give everything to him. My old habits still return and sometimes even my trust is shaken, but ultimately, the reminder of who I am, who he is, and what fulfills me most keeps me surrendering again and again.

I've had to learn to accept who I am in a world filled with people who look at the stereotype of what a slave should be. People read the fantasy slave stories, and I am constantly compared against a generalization I do not fit. I have been told more than once that I am dominant, or that I have power over our relationship. They accept these incorrect views as their truth because of my outgoing and assertive personality, but they do not see what the reality is behind it. I do not fit and I expect I never will. However, as I continue relinquishing power and control, and to be pleasing to Master, life as a slave of strength is as fulfilling as anything else life has to offer. Master accepts me exactly as I am, so I cannot accept myself as anything less than his slave.

About the Author:

slave tanarria, also known as tana by those that know her, is from east central Pennsylvania and has been collared to Master Daniel for nine years in a Master/slave relationship. She is 45 years old and has a 21 year old daughter. tanarria has been with Master Daniel eight of the nine years in a long-distance relationship. They have shared their home together since Master Daniel moved to Pennsylvania from Miami, Florida in November, 2006, to bring their dreams to reality. tanarria is best known throughout the Philadelphia, New York City, Delaware, and central Pennsylvania areas for her vivacious personality, radiant smile, and warm, loving spirit. She is an active member of MAsT Philadelphia, Central NJ MAsT and Northern Delaware Ds (NDDs). She is former owner of the munch group, CentralPennAlt, based in Harrisburg, PA. During her tenure with the munch group, she implemented Discussion Munches and demonstrations, which offered many topics specially geared to those new to the lifestyle. tanarria has been invited to speak as part of the slave track program at the annual Master/slave Conference (MsC) in Washington, DC in August, 2008. She is currently pursuing her Bachelor of Arts Degree in Business Management.

The Art of Obedience

By slave wen

A Parable:

One day a slave arrived at the house of a Master. The slave had spent many years perfecting its slavery through reading and serving many others, attending conferences, and engaging in many forms of submission, pain and sexual activities. Of course, the slave kept finding false Masters, for at some point in each relationship, the Master would ask something of the slave that would surely put the slave in physical or psychological danger, thus requiring the slave to move in search of the "right" Master. The slave kept searching, sure that there was at least one Master worthy of serving and whom would understand and know the slave's needs. After asking around, and seeing many individuals go to one particular Master, the slave was sure this was the house she sought, for the Master had many loyal and dedicated slaves, and was well-respected among other Masters, presenting at conferences, earning many titles and much honor.

After knocking on the door, and requesting to serve in the house, the Master approached this slave. Over many hours and weeks the slave shared its journey with the Master and asked many questions of the Master and slaves. Finally, the slave asked for permission to serve this particular Master. The Master asked the slave a simple question: "What is it that a Master wishes of a slave?" The slave answered, well prepared and eager to serve, "Master, a slave must only obey." The Master replied, "Are you able to obey slave?" The slave assured the Master that it was able to obey. The Master then told the slave that it would be given tasks to complete for that day for preparation of dinner guests. If, after completing those tasks the slave was obedient, the Master would consider the readiness of the slave to begin training. The slave nodded its understanding and awaited dismissal.

Upon leaving the Master's presence, as the slave proceeded in its duties, happy to be obedient, cleaning the Master's house, preparing dinner and completing the various assigned chores, the slave thought upon the meaning of obedience, sure it understood fully what it was to obey. As the slave moved through the day's chores, it decided to cut flowers from the garden to enhance the entryway, sure that the Master would be pleased. Knowing there were guests arriving for dinner, the slave arranged the table in a formal manner, sure that the Master would want to impress the visitors. Additionally, the slave felt that the Master's clothing would need to be cleaned, buffed and laid out, and so the slave added this to the tasks of items to be completed. Even though mopping the kitchen floor was on that day's tasks, the slave felt it was more important for the Master to look good and that the kitchen floor could wait until the next day. The slave was happy in its obedience to the Master's needs. Once the Master returned from errands, the Master entered the house and called the slave to appear before the Master. The slave, anticipating the Master's joy, eagerly presented before the Master. The Master inquired whether the slave had completed all the tasks assigned for that day, and the slave replied, "Master, your slave has completed everything but mopping the kitchen floor." The Master then nodded sadly, and said, "Slave, you have not obeyed. You have much still to learn about obedience."

The slave was most confused, sure that the Master would understand and appreciate the time constraints of the other tasks that were completed in lieu of mopping the kitchen floor. The Master sighed and replied, "Slave, you do not understand what it is to obey fully. If you want the quick path to obedience, you will cut off one of your fingers and present it to my guests. If you can not do that, you may leave my house, and return only when you are ready to present me one of your fingers."

Shocked at the Master's reaction, the slave considered its options and left the house of the Master, sure that the Master was false and crazed for demanding such a drastic action for not mopping the floor, and positive that the Master it sought to serve was never to be found. The slave never returned to that Master's house, and died without ever finding the "right" Master.

In the course of my journey in slavery, the desire to be a fully, completely, and surrendered slave finds conflict with the need to control the parameters and definitions of full, complete, and surrender. I think slaves, like Masters, fear the very thing they want. Slaves struggle with degrees of resistance to surrender and slavery (or, for Masters, Power and Mastery). When slaves approach relationships of surrender, they start with conditions...or limits, as some would say. They set the parameters of the relationship based on mutual agreements and constraints. In these instances, slaves are dabbling in the experience of surrender, but slaves remain on their own terms, thus surrender is a false experience of full surrender; and ultimately, it is unsatisfactory and the slave's needs continue to remain unfulfilled.

I hear many slaves relate the same journey. We begin conversations with the "What ifs" of our fears...what if you wanted me to drink your piss, what if you wanted me to sexually please someone else, what if you wanted me to be naked in front of my family/children?, what if you wanted me to wear a chain around my neck at work where others could see it, what if you wanted me to shave my head, what if you wanted me to wear your permanent mark, what if you wanted me to address you in public as "Master"? When we are told it is not about the what if but about trust, we balk. How can a reasonable, sane person expect us to trust if we don't have the answers to these very important questions? What if you give your trust to some madman or madwoman? What if they decided to kill you, or wanted you to kill yourself?!?

This is, ultimately, the resistance of our ego (our fear) winning the struggle over our wants/desires/needs. We tell ourselves stories and attach to a particular vision of our slave experience so much so that when we are presented the opportunity to experience surrender, we talk ourselves out of it, and deny ourselves achievement of our desire. For example, I was absolutely sure that I knew exactly what type of person I needed for a Master. In searching for that particular Master, I discarded the known for the unknown, and I attached many conditions to my terms of surrender, willing to relinquish those conditions only after "trust" had been earned. I went through Masters like an awards show host goes through outfits. When one Master would demand something unreasonable, I would drop that one and seek another. I displaced my anger and unhappiness onto my husband and conditioned him with poisonous words of inadequacy in meeting my needs as a Master, and I lost valuable time and opportunities because I was so sure I knew what obedience and surrender were supposed to be. These are all false tactics that kept me from experiencing the very thing I needed: full, unconditional surrender. As I arrive at this awareness, I must now acquire new skills of patience, compassion and unconditional acceptance on my part as I try to replant the seeds of Mastery within my husband which my poisonous words supplanted.

I have observed the journey of many Masters and slaves often wends towards one of two main branches: 1) discovering some form of practice and discipline that leads to an understanding of the self in relationship to ego and thus offers the path to surrender, or 2) disillusionment, cynicism, anger and frustration. In both cases, the key seems to be whether an individual is ready and willing to step outside of one's preconceived notions, fear-induced conditions, and self-limiting internalized messages or "tapes". That key is based on one's ability to trust. The trust is not in some "other" or some "Master", but in the "self", and in mastering the "self".

Within all slave's, there is a compulsion towards obedience - the WHAT, WHO and HOW to obey is the remaining mystery for many. In order to fully experience that which the slave most desires (fully surrendering to and obeying a Master) it is essential to first be obedient to one's slave nature by recognizing, honoring and encouraging its fullest expression. It is necessary to eliminate the illusions, fantasies and attachments to the imagined "ideal" slave existence we conjure for ourselves and our Masters.

Resistance to our slave self and to letting go of our attachments has been one of those journeys that I commenced when I first started exploring slavery. Over the years I have observed that even though the answer is given, we don't seem to hear or accept that answer for ourselves. It seems to be part of the path of exploration and self-understanding that must be walked. Some of us will never hear or accept this answer, sure that there is some other, better, path for us. A few will discover the illusions we have constructed and be willing to step through the thresholds of our fears to our destinies and obey the call within.

Thus, I repeat that which has been told to me by many others:

In short: "Be willing to obey absolutely and completely without question."

The longer version: The answer to achieving your deepest desires as a slave (Master) is to be willing to trust yourself enough to fully surrender to your fears without question and obey that which calls you.

About the Author:

slave wen is co-founder of MAsT: Southern Maine, along with her husband and Master, Curtis. Additionally, she hosts a weekly submissives' online chat in Maine, and conducts educational seminars for the Maine Community through the Thorn Society. She is a regular attendee to the Master/slave Conference in Washington, DC, SouthWest Leather Conference in Phoenix, and has attended many other Leather events throughout the years, including Leather Camp, SouthPlains LeatherFest, and Catherine Gross' Servant's Retreat. slave wen considers her slavery part of her spiritual path since the very young age of adolescence. Due to a spiritual calling, she is currently in the process of relocating to Arizona in 2008.

May You Live in Interesting Times: Embracing Life's Changes

By Michelle Smith

I recently read the book "Interesting Times" by Terry Pratchett. For those who have yet to read this book, the title is based on the quote, "May you live in interesting times," which is simultaneously a blessing and a curse. The blessing is to live a life without boredom. The curse is to live a life without any rest. As I look around at my life and the lives of people around me, I definitely believe we live in interesting times.

Slavery can at times be both a blessing and a curse as well. For me, I find both a deep sense of peace and clarity when I have relinquished control. Knowing my Master is capable of making good and just decisions for us both satisfies me in a way that words cannot describe. Slavery can also be a curse and not just because it may require me to scrub the dishes. I have always had an overwhelming need to be in control and to do it all. Relinquishing control, even when I know it will bring me and my Master peace is not always easy.

My Master and I have always held very demanding jobs. As a corporate trainer, I traveled extensively and often worked eighty hours in a week. Though Master was very accommodating of my career and amenable within the constraints it placed upon us, I can see now that my career was also a very effective shield. My career and my attempts to also be overly active in the community actually prevented me from surrendering completely. Surrender takes time and focus, something that cannot happen when one or both parties are overextended.

Last February, I became pregnant with our first child. This blessed event forced us to reprioritize our lives. My Master accepted the change with grace, while I flailed about blindly. My Master says that he prepared for and accepted all that would change the moment we started trying for a family. I, on the other hand, lived in denial until our son was born. Until his birth, I thought I would manage my career, my marriage, my son and also be a slave in my free time. In hindsight, I was out of my hormonally challenged mind.

All physical play stopped when we discovered I was pregnant because even the slightest risk was too great. I am sure many people still play while pregnant, but I don't think either of us would have been able to forgive ourselves if something had happened because I was craving a good caning. Between the mood swings and exhaustion, most of my service stopped as well. This most likely caused more issues than they prevented, but it is difficult to manage a crying, pregnant slave who is rotting in a hotel room three thousand miles away. My Master could have punished me on numerous occasions, but I think he realized I was too irrational for it to have had any corrective effect. No sane woman tells her Master, or anyone for that matter, that he hates his baby for denying his wife stale hotel jelly beans. Fortunately, he didn't take any of my crazy moods personally, which is good since he had a fairly large role in getting me pregnant.

It was difficult and there were protests. Everything was changing so rapidly, and I was in a state of denial. I really didn't think the baby would change our lives that much. I knew we wouldn't attend play parties, but I assumed we would be the same people. I also was scared. I had heard a child would end or drastically dampen the control aspects of our relationship, and I wanted to cling to our previous life. I didn't want to be someone who spent her time remembering "What was." He assured me the control would not change, but my life would.

The absence of routine made giving up control that much more difficult. As I felt the need to cling to control, he started setting out expectations of what would happen after the baby was born. Our lives were going to change and I simply could not accept this. I was queen of doing it all. In college, I took thirty units a quarter, worked between forty and sixty hours a week, was president of a club, volunteered and was engaged to be married. Granted, I was also thirteen years younger and not involved in a power exchange relationship.

Every time, my Master pointed out how our lives were about to change, I balked. I remember arguing with him on the way home from a MAsT meeting. Our chapter was about to have elections and I wanted to run. He told me I was not allowed to run, and I proceeded to argue with him all the way home. More than once, he asked why we were attending a MAsT meeting if I wasn't going to listen to him. He simply wasn't going to allow me to be a slave on my terms. Of course, that type of slavery isn't really slavery and it certainly wouldn't bring me the peace I so desperately need in my life. Sometimes, we truly are our own worst enemy, struggling against the very thing that will bring us happiness.

The struggles continued on and off until our son was born. Some of the struggles were hormonally based, and some were based on my fears that everything was going to change. I have never faced change very well, even when that change was planned. It is something I am working on, with his help.

One of the reasons I serve my Master is because he has a foresight that I sometimes lack. With the birth of our son came many changes. I no longer travel the world for work. Instead, I work from home. This change has allowed us to start to institute much of the structure we had only dreamed about before. Having me home every day allows my Master the freedom to plan and to provide structure. We still need to be flexible as every day with our son is different; but even so, there is now continuity.

As he had predicted, I also changed. Hospitals must give very good drugs during childbirth because when our son was born, all my fears, all my mood swings and all my fight vanished. I, once again, found the desire to serve, to listen and to obey.

My desires for structure and control have also increased tremendously. I want to feel his power and strength, and I want to do everything I can for our family. As I surrender more to him, I have a much greater peace in my life. Though I always obeyed, I would often argue if I didn't agree. I don't seem to argue as much, except during those sleep deprived moments where we both grate on each other's nerves. We've realized that those moments are really a sign that we need to take a few minutes to reconnect, with me at his feet or my head in his lap.

I am not the only one who has changed. I don't know if it is having me home each night, my increased desire to serve him more fully, or simply watching the miracle of our son, but my Master has become increasingly confident these past two months. Before our son was born, I was afraid the lack of events would cause us to become apathetic about our Master/ slave dynamic, but his increased confidence has caused us both to focus on the power exchange much more intensely. For the first time in our lives, our priorities seem to match our desires, something not always easy to achieve.

It sounds odd but, the power exchange dynamic in our relationship has strengthened since the birth of our son. The fast paced outside world no longer matters. If I miss a phone call, an e-mail, or an event, I simply don't care. Our son has caused us both to refocus and reprioritize our lives and what is really important to us. Though I still enjoy socializing, it has taken a distant second to doing things to serve my Master and to tend to our son.

By focusing on our relationship and our family, I have started to let go in ways I had never even considered before and as I relinquish more and more control, I grow. I grow as his wife and as his slave. I wouldn't recommend having a baby simply to increase the power dynamic in a relationship, but having a baby definitely doesn't have to be the end of it. Sometimes, you simply need to accept life's many changes and use the change as an opportunity to assess where you are in your relationship and where you want to be in your career, your social obligations, and your commitments until they do. If they aren't the same place, then reprioritize.

About the Author:

Michelle, an avid Redskins' fan, has lived in the suburbs of Philadelphia since the end of 1999. In 2006, she married her Master, Jeff. Jeff and Michelle recently welcomed their first born son into the world. Her interests in the lifestyle have grown over past decade and with the birth of their son, Jeff and Michelle are now developing a more comprehensive household manual to help both partners grow. She is a member of both Philadelphia and Central New Jersey MAsT and a local support group for submissives. Though she may not be able to attend as many events with the newborn, she does try to maintain contact with those in the community so she can continue to learn from their experiences. In addition to serving her Master, Michelle also serves two demanding cats. Michelle enjoys a wide range of hobbies from gaming to cooking to a plethora of crafts. Michelle has an intense passion for learning and is constantly seeking ways to learn and to grow both as an individual and as a slave. Balancing work, love, family and the lifestyle can be challenging, but is also extremely rewarding

Serviculture - The Art of Cultivating the Slave Mind

By *slave namaste*

Horticulture is the art of cultivating a garden, in the same vein "serviculture" - from the Latin serv- for servant or slave, and culture meaning to cultivate- is my coined term for the art of cultivating the slave. In this piece I'd like to focus on the art of cultivating the slave mind specifically. While there are other areas of cultivation in regard to slavery (the physical self, the spirit of the slave, the skills of the slave etc.), I have found no area that needs such constant diligence as the slave mind.

The slave mind simply by being unseen is somewhat of a "secret" garden. It can be a place of great depth and perception, a place full of many flowers to delight the senses of any Master. It can also be a place full of vines of doubt, poison of past pain and quicksand of insecurity. Like any garden, even the best slave mind will become overrun by weeds and undesirable traits if not cultivated. There are a number of factors involved in cultivation, an examining of the aspects involved and their practical application can be extremely helpful in the M/s dynamic.

Plowing - Plowing is the turning over, loosening and digging up of soil. It is how you loosen the ground and prepare it to receive fertilizer, seed etc.; It is what must be done so that soil becomes soft and receptive. As this pertains to the slave mind, it is the process of the slave revealing his/her mind to the Owner/Master. It is the slave being transparent and open in expressing past experiences, hurts and traumas. The greatest tool in plowing being trust. The greater the slaves trust in the Owner the more transparent the slave will be. It is also the slave sharing with the Owner or Master his/her ideas, perspectives and philosophies in a very open and honest way. There are of course things the Master/ Owner can do to facilitate this. Directly asking the slave to speak about specific situations from his/her past, or perspectives on current experiences is one way. Journaling can also be a good way to encourage transparency. This process of plowing also speaks to unearthing ideas that are potentially in conflict with those of the Owner. Long discussions can facilitate this. These discussions may be planned but they can often take place when a stone is "accidentally" unearthed. Better to dig it up when it is found than to continually stub one's toe on it!

Fertilizing and amending - This is applying some needful mineral or supplement to the soil that helps it become more productive. It is a way of adding nutrients that the soil is deficient in. In the art of serviculture, this can take the form of the addition of traits such as patience, grace, or education to the slave. This can mean having the slave take classes to learn new ideas or ways of thinking. There are various types of education that activate different places in the mind. There are activities which can help the slave become a secure and well rounded person. Spending time in active pursuit of various kinds of learning can be a worthwhile endeavor for a slave. It is important to note that fertilization in this context is not planting. Fertilization is adding amendments which compliment and aid in what is to be planted ...not the addition of things which compete with the seeds planted. One will need to be very aware of the type of "garden" one has to know what type of fertilizer to use.

Planting - Why do we do all of the plowing and fertilizing? So that we can plant. In the slave mind, this means inserting those ideas into the slave psyche which you desire to develop slaves can be like sponges ready and able to absorb anything that gets close to them. Masters can take advantage of this by planting thoughts, ideas, and concepts in the slave which they seek to develop more fully. Because a slave is a reflection of his/her Owner, this is a wonderful opportunity for the Master/Mistress to *actively* participate in the development of the slave. If one desires for the slave to be demure, planting seeds of brattiness will likely not yield the desired result. Just as in a garden, when planting be conscious of the desired end, and the "space" requirements for the crop. Planting seeds of "high protocol" slavery when one intends to live a very casual life with very casual interactions between Master and slave will only frustrate the slave and annoy the Master in the long run. Also note the abilities of the slave. slaves vary greatly as to how many new concepts they can effectively "hold" and internalize at any one time. Planting too many new things can result in ideas which never reach maturity due to having a very shallow root system. (Beware of planting an ocean of ideas which are only an inch deep)

Tending - In tending we're dealing with being watchful. Watchful over what is growing in the slave mind, and watchful over debris and such which can accumulate and cause problems. The most fertile rich soil can still become a wasteland if one allows weeds to grow and leach precious energy away from the plants. There are two basic types of trash - internal and external. External trash consists of things which come from outside. Being watchful for ideas and perspectives which are not conducive to slavery prevents them from taking firm root and jeopardizing the garden. Many times a slave will be distracted and thrown off course by ideas she comes across online or by developing a preoccupation with others' dynamics for instance. Internal trash consists of things that come from within the slave. I believe Thich Nhat Hanh said it best, "The garden always produces garbage. If you are an organic gardener, you know how to handle the garbage. You know the techniques of transforming the garbage back into compost and into flowers. You don't have to throw away anything at all. So, the energy of fear, of anger should be considered to be the garbage. Let it be produced, because it can become the art of mindful living. So, now we should learn how to handle the garbage in us, namely, craving, anger, fear and despair. We should not be afraid of the garbage in us if we know how to transform it back into joy, into peace." From this we see that even the internal trash can be transformed into something good for the soil (and the slave!) if handled properly. Internal trash can serve as a revealer of the slaves thought process and can aid in training the slave. There is a balance there.

Training - This is a topic that we hear spoken of a great deal. For the sake of this article we're speaking of the training of the slave mind. When one seeks to train a grape vine it involves a number of aspects. Cutting off vines that do not produce but suck energy away from those vines that are productive is one of the outcomes of training. Bending and twisting vines to the desired shape or to adhere to the necessary support systems is another. So too with the slave mind, a slave may begin to pursue various rabbit trails. It may be necessary to curtail these pursuits in favor of the Owners main focus at that time. The slaves thoughts may need to be focused and shaped to assume the shape the Master desires or encouraged to continue to grow in the direction he or she is seeking. Just as with plants such training is accomplished more easily when the thoughts are young, so vigilance is preferred. However this is not to say that old tapes can not be done away with, just that it may take more time and a firmer touch to train the mind to go in a different direction if the current internal thought pattern is long standing. Be assured that such commitment is often well worth it!

Promote growth, foster - One must know what one is attempting to grow in order to know how to nurture and foster said growth. Different attitudes and perspectives require different care. Training for domestic service is very different than training to be a pony girl. Once one knows what traits are valuable and needful, doing things to create a nurture environment for that growth to take place can make all the difference between a slave that is confident in his/her abilities or a slave who is insecure and stunted in their growth. Water and sunshine in the form of praise, stimulation and emotional support are necessary for the growth of the seeds planted.

Harvesting - Serviculture is not punitive in nature. It is not only about the prevention of the negative but also about harvest; after all, that is why we plant, fertilize and do all that we do. It would be a travesty to do all of the necessary preparation only to have the fruit rot on the vine because it has not been harvested. How does one harvest the slave mind? By recognizing the desirable traits and actively using them. Still water tends to stagnate. There are many ways to use the bounty of the slave mind. Teaching others is a good way as it harvests what one has as well as helping in other gardens! Giving in service to the community, one's Leather Family, or one's Owner are excellent ways to harvest the bounty. Allowing the slave to be involved in activities which will actively utilize the traits that have been cultivated will often help increase his/her self esteem and confidence. Slaves tend to thrive on making their Owners proud and using the training and guidance they have received from their Owner is something most slaves enjoy.

In the end, it's all about forming the slave and refining

the slave into the best they can be. The mind has been called a battlefield and the one true barrier to the Master. With cultivation, it can also become a wonderful ally in the quest for slavery.

About the Author:

slave namaste has counseled women and taught about embracing submission for over 12 years. She brings this knowledge into her relationship serving as Master Obsidians' 24/7 TPE slave as well as to counseling and aiding in the development of other slaves in the lifestyle. Her writings on surrender and absolute slavery have been featured on web sites and e-zines. She is Founder and co-moderator of various lifestyle groups including one geared specifically for slaves in TPE relationships and another for Austin, TX Area Ladies in Kink. She has a focus on Servitude, Femininity, Protocols, Spirituality and The Art of Surrender.

The Collar

By slave tanarria

Reaching up to touch her neck

empty

a soft gasp escapes her lips

missing

There should be the link

the chain, the bond,

the never ending circle

of life, of love

Sadness fills her eyes

her soul empty

it cries out

to the loss, the dread

the lesson learned

kneeling

tears streaming down her cheeks

crying, harsh sobs choke her words

she begs to return to honor

to love, to serve, to him

He looks down upon her

tears filling his own eyes

love in his heart, hurt in his soul

He kneels beside her, touching her chin

lifting her eyes to his,

a soft kiss to her lips

The clasp undone,

the chain slips around her neck

fastened forever

in a circle of love, of life

of slavery, of ownership

She lays her head in his lap

He gently strokes her hair

tears soak their bodies

the bond is returned

to its rightful place

around the slave's neck

and the Master's heart

PEBRS

The expectation of fairness

By Danae Casen

I had one of those days recently where, when I finally got into bed my body just gave a big sigh of relief. I had gotten up early to clean, to bake and to do all the things I typically do each day but in the midst of it all, there were many other little things that needed to be done. So I was on my feet from the time I got up until I hit the bed. Before going to sleep, I decided to pick up the book I had been reading and I had one of those moments where I had to remind myself it is an erotic "fairy tale." You see, I am rereading *The Claiming of Sleeping Beauty* by A. N. Roquelaure (aka Anne Rice).

The book is perfect fairy tale porn. The slave has a groom that bathes her in scented oils, does her hair and make up, lotions and massages her body after long night of kinky fun and sex. He does many other things to the slave that sound like she is at a spa being pampered instead of having a typical day I've been having as a slave (at least in my opinion.) She has kinky fun in many different ways, and is of course having quite a lot of sex because she is always a wet needy slut. It is a rarity in the book when you see Beauty, the main character, doing every day mundane chores such as laundry, scrubbing the toilet, making the bed or dusting the living room. And of course Beauty is always in the mood for sex and ready to please her Owner.

But here I am, lying in bed, feeling the ache of my muscles after a long day of work and chores. So when I read a slave that is being pampered, having lots of kinky fun and sex, yes, I can admit that my little voice of --- "It's not fair" kicked in.

Over the past 5 years, I have had that voice come up now and again during service to my Owner. It is not something I am proud of but it happens.

"He gets to lounge on the couch while I finish cleaning up at dinner. It isn't fair. "

"He gets to go have a beer with friends. And I have to stay home and wash the floor. It isn't fair."

"I don't even drink coffee- why do I have to clean the coffee pot out? It isn't fair."

"He gets to go to bed and I need to finish folding clothes. I am tired... why can't I be in bed? It isn't fair."

"I want to have chicken for dinner but he wants meatloaf. It isn't fair. "

"He can buy a video game and I have to ask for permission to buy a little lipstick. It isn't fair."

Each of those are lines has gone through my brain. Yes, I am a slave. Yes, I understand what it means to be a slave. Yet it is one of those ouch moments, full of negative emotion and frustration. It can be hard to remember all the reasons why slavery is very gratifying to me in the turmoil of emotions.

I have read the Beauty books a few times over the years, but I still remember the first time I read them. I was early in my discovery that there were many people out in the world like me and desiring a Master/slave relationship. Yes, the Beauty books are based on a fairy tale, but I won't deny that when reading the books, there was a part of me that wished that I would get used like Beauty does in the books. Even knowing that the story was just fairy tale still didn't stop those fantasies coming to my mind.

It also made me stretch it into my own fantasies of what a perfect day in my life as a slave would be like. I thought of the days and nights I would spend being locked in a cage, being scantily clad or naked 24 hours a day, 7 days a week for the pleasure of my Master and just all the kinky fun stuff like spankings, bondage and sex while gagged or hooded. I am not saying that we don't do those things, nor am I saying that we don't have a lot of fun doing those things. But we just can't do those things 365 days because the cable guy needs into the house next Wednesday to do repairs, vanilla friends are stopping by tomorrow to borrow a book, that pile of laundry in the hamper won't wash itself, and those meals don't magically appear on the dinner table. I think I sometimes got so caught up in the story - the fantasy that I came to believe that once in a Master/slave relationship, everything domestic and mundane magically happens or instantly becomes erotic and you get to have fun kinky sex 24/7. I'd like to think I am a fairly well grounded person, but I know that a little part of me thought that now my life would be amazingly erotic and glamorous every day of the year.

I always knew there would be some level of domestic service in my life as slave, but really how often did that enter my mind way back when dreaming of a Master/slave relationship? Well about as much as Beauty does domestic service in *The*

Claiming of Beauty – meaning very little. In my *reality*, being a slave has a lot more vanilla than not and that is the rub and struggle of slavery at times. There are parts of domestic service that I actually kind of like. It is just that sometimes the everyday vanilla stuff starts becoming routine – too mundane. And when things start getting to be so mundane and routine it can be very easy to fall into the "It's not fair" mode. It's a struggle. But it's a different kind of struggle then the kind when I wince and writhe when I see Master's hand rise up ready to slap my clothespin covered breasts, and it might be a bit of a struggle to stand still. It's a different struggle than when I don one of the hoods, gasping, anticipating and struggling in the confines of the darkness. The struggle of what is fair falls into its own category because it's an internal struggle I might be fighting against myself in defiance of the essence of my slavery. So after floating in glow of masochism– that struggle isn't remembered. But having to cook dinner, weed the flowerbeds, do the laundry or scrub the floor after a hard long day -- that is where the real struggle happens. It reminds me that we have responsibilities in our life when I want our Master/slave relationship to be all erotic and glamorous.

When negative emotions and frustrations hit and things become mundane and routine, I know I need to move past it. Because if I let those feelings take control, all of those resentments will build and bitterness will become an apparent immediate negative reaction to everyday tasks, work and chores. The "It's not fair" struggle is a very human state. What is important is to find ways to move past it so that it doesn't interfere with my service and/or attitude towards my service.

Usually, when I realize I have been having a case of "It's not fair," I slow things down to think about why I am feeling those emotions. Typically, it is just that I am tired and had a long day. That doesn't always make it easier, but being aware and reminding myself of why it hit at times does help step back from the situation. Taking a few deep breaths and then reminding myself of who I am, why I am here, and what I get out of it is a way to help me work through the frustration and negativity. Something else that helps me is looking at it from a different perspective. Because, when I slow down and think about what proves to me that I am slave more - being locked in a cage, flogged and hooded verses being on my hands and knees washing Master's kitchen floor while he is sitting in the living room watching a movie with a iced coffee that I just delivered to him moments before. Hands down (no pun intended) being on my knees and washing the kitchen floor while he relaxes are a great reminder that I am slave. It reminds me who I am, why I am here and what I get out of this journey. At the end of the day I finally arrive at a place of where I am at in my journey – a slave.

Because the reality of this journey is I ultimately enjoy seeing Master be able to lounge on the couch after he has had a long hard day while I wash the floor, do laundry or dishes. It makes me feel good. It is very gratifying knowing I am able to serve him freeing up his time to relax. And that is the moment I realize how I am very much in the place I have always really wanted as a slave and in ways that are beyond the fantasy, erotica and porn. Because I am not Master's peer, I am his slave to serve him. And more importantly I want to be his slave. I want to serve him and have that service enhance his life.

About the Author:

Danae lives in western Colorado and has been in a service oriented M/s relationship with Michael for the last 5 years. Before moving to Colorado, she lived in Ohio where she was active in several BDSM organizations through volunteering her time. In her free time, she creates art, enjoys day trips around beautiful Colorado and frequently gets lost in books from many different genres. She has written for newsletters, contributed to websites and reflects on her own journey in the lifestyle in an online blog. For more information about Danae, please visit www.withinreality.com

Slave Heaven

By Tina Sweet

During every waking moment that I am not in His presence, I don a disguise. It is one that displays impressive independence. It is decorated with confidence, perseverance, and self assuredness, even power. When I catch a glimpse of my disguise in a mirror, I am impressed and amused. How do I do it? How do I soar with ease while weighed down by countless layers that bury my ever present true self? Underneath the disguise lives a perpetual panic, and an uneasiness buried deep within. I feel like something is missing or lost. I feel like there's an empty space in me. No matter how I've tried to rid myself of the panic, it remains and follows me where ever I go. I could spend a lifetime trying to trace its roots. There have been times when I've wondered when and why I designed my disguise. One could blame it on my upbringing, or on my failed relationships, or genetics, but to me it's irrelevant. I am His now.

The moment he arrives- as soon as I hear the turning doorknob, I am doused with comfort. I start breathing again with a gasp of relief. My eyes are open and I am alive. I am at ease inside. The perpetual panic dissipates. To witness this sudden conversion would shock any outsider. Now that he is here, I am a coveted child. The disguise, the mask, and all the layers that weigh me down are torn apart exposing body and soul as soon as he opens the door. As he walks in the world spins just a bit slower and allows me to dwell in the exalting height of pure joy. Each time my heart beats this joy is brand new again. I take my place in this safe haven that has been created just for me. The perpetual panic and its warriors weaken and retreat. They take a needed break to prepare for the next attack, but I am not concerned with battle. I just relish in the relief. When he arrives, I don't even think about the perpetual panic, and I don't feel it leaving. Its tyranny is erased from existence. His presence is my redemption, my pardon. My prison door subtly loosens from its hinges. He takes his little girl by the hand and leads her out. This relief takes control of every part of me. I know nothing but him. I only feel, see, want, need Master.

My safe haven is at his feet. There's an intense longing in me that never seems to wane. No matter how long I remain, it's never long enough. My soul rests quietly, and the rush of relief pours down like rain on a parched dry desert. What peaceful refuge his presence is. With my head in his lap, he gently strokes my hair and runs his fingers through until he has a firm grip. He lifts my head and allows my eyes to meet his. His eyes are the most beautiful eyes I've seen. I am captured by his stare and I have never felt so free. I wonder how I was ever upright and conscious without him. I don't remember what that was like. And honestly, I have no desire to.

He can look right through me, deep into me, and know my thoughts and hear my hopes of what will occur next. My silence speaks to him in a language that was created by some part of me that I can't identify. It's a part that was undiscovered but ever-present throughout my whole life. He uncovered this buried treasure as though he knew where it was all along. It is as though he could see it clear as day the very second he knew I would be his little girl. I believe that there are occurrences in life which words cannot be created for. They would fall absurdly short. Perhaps things like this should remain sacred, unspoken, beyond verbal description. What exudes from the deepest part of my existence calls out to Master in a language is one that no one else can understand.

He knows me like he knows his own name. There is nothing about me that startles him. The poisoned parts of me are purified with His firm hand or his stinging whip. He cleanses these parts with his soothing touch and his consuming embrace. All the things I hide from the rest of the world are exposed to him without reluctance. My hopes, fantasies, desires, dreams, encompass him. Although I've only spoken a few out loud, he knows all of them. He knows my every morbid thought, and adores me still. His hands and his instruments have touched and tortured every inch of flesh. My body is his, and he takes it with great delight. I unabashedly reveal every part of me, and suddenly, my physical flaws that I loathe are unnoticeable to my own eyes. For a moment, I see myself through his. I see a graceful divine desired woman. I am breathtaking. I am his deepest desire, his strongest lust, his prized possession. With fierce aggression, he seizes every part of me. I relish in this privilege. He claims me as his prize over and over again. I come to life. Restrained, bruised, invaded, broken, yet free and whole.

While words fail to express so much, there are three that bring me to a place of ecstasy. He whispers them softly. He says them with a wry sinister smile. He yells with aggression in his booming voice. He presses his lips hard against my ear and speaks them clear. I can be resting in his lap. I can be chained, bound, suspended in air. I can be walking beside him. And no matter where I am in what fashion they come from his lips, they bring me to my place:

"You are mine."

About the Author:

Tina lives just a stone's throw from the ocean on the lovely NJ shore. She is in a new M/s relationship with her Daddy Dom after being "ownerless" for way too long. She is a published author and successful business woman; however, her true passion lies in being a good girl and becoming the best pleasure slave for her Daddy. She is an adoring mother of 3. She is an accomplished seamstress who expects to use her skills to design lifestyle accessories, furniture, apparel, etc. in the future. Tina is an endurance athlete and will run her first marathon this fall. She and her Daddy do not attend lifestyle events at this time as they prefer to indulge in each other exclusively whenever time allows. She plans to attend educational lifestyle events once she is refined and tamed by her delicious Master.

Serving a Master with Feet of Clay

By Michelle Smith

New relationships are filled with such hope and promise; they are almost intoxicating. When a relationship first begins, everything is unknown. Each day becomes Christmas with a thousand presents to unwrap, and each new discovery leads to still more gifts. New relationships also offer the opportunity for each person to be on their best behavior and to be at their best.

When a relationship is still fresh, it is quite easy to put your dominant partner on a pedestal. They may seem ominous, always in control, frightening, powerful or even god-like. Though aspects of these qualities might exist in the dominant, most often they are merely projections of the slave's own desires. Dominants also can project unrealistic expectations on their new submissive partners.

The pressure to please a dominant and to live up to

their standards, regardless of what those standards are is tremendous in those early moments. When talking to slaves, many will indicate that the worst punishment is the knowledge that they disappointed their partner. In a new relationship, what will disappoint is unknown so people often try a little harder. Not only do they try harder, but both parties may be so caught up in the moment that they overlook small missteps. This combination only furthers the illusion of who the other person really is – mythology compared to reality.

The combination of the unknown and unbridled hope can lead some people to outperform themselves, to push themselves to an unsustainable level in hopes of being pleasing, and even to make decisions they would not under other circumstances. When the "new relationship smell" starts to fade and the illusion disappears, it can leave both parties in a quandary about how to proceed.

My Master is someone who enjoys pushing limits, and I have a deep need to please. The combination can lead to some very powerful and rewarding play. When I look back to the early stages of our relationship, I was driven to be the unbelievably perfect slave. Anything he desired, I worked to achieve. If he did something that would cause me to quirk a brow, I would quickly dismiss it. I didn't want to rock the boat. I even managed to keep my often fiery temper in check, managing to never become upset regardless of what was happening. I had an image of who he was as a dominant and who I should be as a submissive and did everything I could to keep that image a reality.

Those early months were quite exciting. I experienced new things, some of which I never would have tried with an existing partner. I explored new avenues in my submission and a desire to serve. Granted, I still don't like doing dishes or changing the cat box, but there are many other aspects to myself that only surfaced during that "try-everything" stage of the new relationship. As someone who enjoys breaking through boundaries and exploring limits, my Master was like a child in a candy store.

It was a heady experience and it caused us to act quite impetuously at times. Master offered and I accepted his collar on our six month anniversary when we were still very much entrenched in the "new" stage of our relationship and when everything was still perfect. I typically don't recommend people jump into collaring or accept someone's collar before there has been at least one argument, disagreement or stumbling block that was overcome. Despite rushing into the collaring, it was still something we both took quite seriously, and it is probably the reason we are still together- now married and enjoying many sleepless nights due to our first son.

During our initial interactions, I managed to overlook potential issues. I was so enthralled by being pushed, controlled and owned in new ways that I pretended to not see his baggage. I ignored everything that threatened my perspective of my Master and our relationship - because how can you serve someone with flaws?

A few months after I was collared, a previous mistake of my Masters' had a tremendous, and at the time, very negative impact on our relationship. Not only was I faced with this one mistake, but the hundred other little issues suddenly came to the forefront of my mind. The image of the man who was so much greater than I am was shattered. I saw a man with flaws and I feared that the relationship was forever ruined as I watched him slip off the pedestal; a pedestal I had placed him on, based on expectations he eventually would not have been able to meet.

Had I not worn his collar, I would have slipped into my old patterns and abandoned the relationship. It would have been the easy thing to do, but a collar to me is a promise to give all that you can. I tried to return to my blissful ignorance and simply not see the problem but that didn't work. Fortunately, it taught us both that open communication is really critical to the success or failure of a relationship. The more we communicated, the more we grew as individuals and more importantly as Master and slave.

Though communication strengthened our relationship into something stronger than it was, the idealistic image I once had of my Master was forever shattered. I knew that he was a man who had flaws, who made mistakes and had weaknesses- just like I did. I feared this knowledge would decrease the strength of my submission to him - and for a while it did. I struggled with how to serve a man who made mistakes, knowing he would continue to make them.

As we moved past our issues, the unknowing awe and fear I once had of him faded, but with time it was replaced with something much stronger- respect.

Our communication can at times be brutal. I know many who carefully phrase every word and while that works for many, it didn't work for us. We weren't able to move from the honeymoon period of our relationship into a period of acceptance until we learned to be who we naturally are. For me, I need to express what is on my mind and I need to know that it is heard plainly. I also need to hear the blunt truth from my Master, even if I don't like it at the time. Anything else risks us becoming involved with the illusion of who we believe the other person to be, instead of reality.

It's easy to give yourself to a perfect illusion, but it's not realistic nor is it long lasting. Though I enjoyed the thrill of the new relationship, I have found myself sustained and satisfied as a slave by serving someone whose flaws I see. Watching my Master ponder the next step we take or watch him struggle to make a decision that will benefit both of us for the long term is awe-inspiring. Witnessing his angst the one time he had to punish me was very humbling, and it made me try harder to be mindful of any rules or expectations he established. Knowing that he will make mistakes and learn from them, and that I am allowed the same luxury, has lead me to take chances and propose things I wouldn't have otherwise. Instead of just waiting for him to act, I share deeper fantasies, ideas I'd like to explore, and I feel safe to bare myself completely. I can tell him how I struggle with some of his decisions and we can talk about how to move past them.

Knowing my Master has feet of clay allows me to serve more fully, and to grow to become a better slave and ultimately a better human being. Instead of the illusion, I serve the man he is. And instead of forcing myself to do new things out of fear, I do them now because the Master I serve has earned the right to make those choices for me and for us.

The Art of Transparency

By slave wen

I am always intrigued by the concept of transparency as it relates to the power dynamic within Mastery and slavery. I hear many people adamantly adhere to the belief that slaves must always be transparent while Masters are held to a lesser degree of what constitutes transparency because it is viewed as necessary for the power exchange for Masters to be allowed to withhold thoughts, information and decisions from slaves.

In my opinion, this belief promotes ineptitude in Masters and fosters poor understanding of power-based relationship building. I don't seek slavery in order to be screwed without an orgasm. I already experience that with the current political administration's policies of "don't ask, don't tell" and getting misinformed daily on a "need to know" basis. I don't want this with a Master as well! I seek slavery as a pathway towards my own self-realization and full potentiation. I also think that Masters are drawn to mastery for the same reason - at least on some level, whether it is conscious or not.

Transparency within the context of Master/slave relationships is first and foremost about doing the work on one's self in stripping away the ego, the stories, and the projections of self and others until we are able to be in a place of non-judgment, compassion and acceptance with all of what makes us "be" in this moment. This is essentially a whole-life project for most of us, excepting the few enlightened Ones, of course - which means "you" - right? Discounting an immediate "mastery" of this process, transparency then requires development of self-knowledge with regard to emotion, thought, observation, judgment, reaction, and acceptance.

In my experience, very few Masters and slaves have achieved success in the realm of complete self-knowledge and mastery of emotion, thought, observation, judgment, reaction and acceptance. In order to achieve these skill sets, one is required to engage in relationship. Those of us in Master/slave relationships have chosen to do this with relation to power.

Because slaves are required to be transparent in feeling, thought, observation, and reactions, the process of self-learning and development is facilitated through the power dynamic. When we do not also require this of Masters, there is a great risk of asynchronous development and stagnation of personal development of the Master. Thus, the belief system that states it is necessary for slaves to be transparent, but it is acceptable and even necessary for Masters to "not be", is inherently flawed and subject to creating relationship discord as a result of uneven degrees of self-knowledge. It sets relationships up for failure because the power it is based upon is unequal and held unaccountable.

While this particular dynamic may be the majority of relationships in Master/slave power dynamics, it may also be the core issue for why so many relationships last only a few years.

If one looks to the spiritual practices of transparency, those who lead and teach also spend a great deal of time on developing self-understanding. They spend a great deal of effort in understanding the role of ego in terms of our attachments. It is my belief that transparency when practiced equally by Master and slave allows for genuine growth and full potentiating of all individuals. In Asian martial arts, when the student asks the Master a question, the student expects the Master to answer from a place of personal insight, experience and wisdom. This can only occur with a Master willing to ask those same questions of himself and willing to seek the answers.

Now for those of you already jumping on your high horses about some rebel slave upsetting the apple cart, I ask that you bear with me. I am not suggesting that we require our Masters to share all the deep, inner secrets and reveal the evilness of their "Master" plans for us. I am asking for slaves to hold your Masters to a standard of personal accountability in words, deed and actions. I admit that I have been less than slave-like in my own personal history of telling my Master when he was an idiot and of pointing out just how un-Master-like he was. I can also tell you that it makes for two unhappy people. I felt un-slave-like in direct proportion to how much I told him he was being un-Master-like. Neither of us were happy...and both were frustrated. So there are ways in which to accomplish being a slave and holding the Master accountable for being transparent.

Some of my own personal experience lessons include:

1) Speak the truth as you see it and seek clarification on your viewpoint. "I do not see the Master in you when you keep allowing the same behaviors from that particular slave to upset you. Are you giving away your power to that slave?" or "I feel like you are trying to please me and not yourself when you wait

for me to decide our social agenda. Are you giving away your power to me in this situation?" This works much better than, "You are not the Master for me. You let me have too much control!"

2) Acknowledge in your truth-speaking when you have an attachment or agenda and then ask for insight and sharing. "I am disappointed in your decision to stay home tonight because I thought it would be a good opportunity to promote your vision. What are your plans in communicating your vision?" This works much better than "I am always setting up opportunities and you never take them." or "We never go anywhere!" and then spending the evening flumping around and being resentful of doing foot massages at your Master's feet!

3) Be willing to openly experiment with your communication styles and to practice with one another using non-confrontational language. An excellent resource is the book by Laurie Weiss. This is a business book, but is an excellent example of using the power dynamic of how to speak to your "boss" as an employee. Slaves can gain a lot from this book in how to address the Master using respect while maintaining the power dynamic.

Even as I continue to wrestle with this concept called transparency, I still remain wary of Masters whom are not willing to be transparent in sharing thoughts, observations, reactions and personal insights from lessons learned along the way. I suppose I find it hard to serve a Master not willing to put in the same effort as is requested of me. Perhaps if more slaves demanded transparency of Masters we'd have a lot less "disingenuous" and a lot more "genuine" Masters available.

Serving as a Geisha

By Evy

The story of this part of my journey started about Christmas time, two years ago. I was not totally new to the lifestyle. My heart had already acquired a few bumps and bruises along my path. But on this day, something that I had been dreaming of for quite a long time, finally happened. I met a Dominant.... in real life... Who took me out for a lunch date!

O. K. So a lunch date may not sound so extraordinary for some of those who will read this; but for me, it was. My ex husband was my ex because he never courted me. My previous Master lived too far away to bother with frivolities. The rare occasions when I had seen his face in person had been for 'specific' reasons. I had even been courted by one of the most sincere and gentle Dominants I have ever met... long distance. So a casual lunch was almost unheard of.

For as much as I know I should not have gone, but I decided to go with the flow after enjoying our meal and allowed the new Dominant to take me for a drive. With the sun shining high and my clothes still on, I was as much thankful as I was nervous. When I finally got the courage to explain to him that I wished to know what he desired of my time, he said "right now, young lady, your job is to sit there and look beautiful."

Me... Beautiful? Granted, I had learned that confidence in my own sexuality was desirable. Over the years, I had learned to dress myself in a flattering way. From childhood, I had been encouraged to carry myself in an elegant manner. More recently, I had been trained to groom myself that my inner fire would shine through my eyes. I had even learned to look at myself in the mirror (while nude) and smile. But, to sit there and "look beautiful," was a challenge. One, I felt inadequately trained for. A short time later, I was introduced to "Aos". At that time, my mind felt like I had found another piece to my puzzle. The next piece was to be Nawa Tatu's Geisha files.

See, this girl is a firm believer in that we all must walk our own path. We all have our own puzzles to build that reflect our inner soul and help us to understand who and what we are meant to be as we strive to become the best that we (as individuals) can be. The forks in the road that we accept grant us another colorful tile that we may place as we see fit. It is here that I have been granted an opportunity to share with you a few of the pieces I have gathered along my path.

From Aos, I have learned that granting your heart and soul in service as a slave can be a beautiful form of art. That a girl (or boy) can put forth the extra effort to make the simplest task a thing of beauty. Some say that it is one thing to serve and another to serve well, those of us on Aos live those words every day. For service is about more than obeying when told to kneel. It is about smiling as you present a plate full of food and remembering all the favorite condiments. It is about having the place settings arranged in a pleasing manner. It is about the extra details like fresh flowers, hot tea and music being played in the background. It is about creating a beautiful, relaxing and harmonious atmosphere for those you serve.

The true history of the word "Geisha" is actually quite interesting. As far back as the 1600s Geisha First began to enter the pleasure districts home to Yujo. Yujo is the Japanese word for a trained and licensed sex professional. Where as a Geisha is an artist. Originally the musicians, jesters and actors were all male, per society's expectations at that time. Eventually, women were permitted to take up the arts and also work for a living as a professional Geisha. Now, Geisha are known for their strict discipline in maintaining the historical traditions of their art.

How does this relate to my place as a slave under the umbrella of the leather lifestyle? I feel Nawa Tatu put it very well when he said "The word 'geisha' literally means "beautiful or artistic person". The geisha is a very intelligent and educated woman. She is one who is skilled in the arts of providing a fantasy. She has been schooled to make ones dreams come true, she has a gift to make the unreal real. She is an entertainer, she plays music, she sings, she dances. She is a poet, an artist with arranging flowers. She can converse with great knowledge and intelligence in virtually all subject matters, whether it be politics, business or pleasure." Include the thought that "As a submissive, a personal geisha to your sensei, you have a responsibility to bring a love and harmony to your environment. It is a geisha's pleasure to introduce beauty in to the household." It was when I read those words that I knew I had found where I belonged.

But I did not even find that first. I actually stumbled on the Ds-arts web sight when seeking to learn more about my passionate desire for rope. I wanted to learn how to enjoy rope in a beautiful, meditative, and platonic way. I wanted to learn more of what my friends referred to as Shibari. The way of the rope drew me into a spiritual view of BDSM that I had been craving, seeking, needing to find. This was the balance I had been yearning for. A way in which to find peace out of passion. The more I began to see the beauty and serenity in the form of Power Exchange I desired the most, the more I began to appreciate how beautiful it could be to serve... and in more than just one way.

One example of a skill I have yet to acquire is that of tea. Greatly due to geography, opportunities and resources to study the way of Tea are difficult to come across. I honestly can not remember where I read it, but there is a description regarding the principals of the tea ceremony. The Author was describing all the work involved in preparing a traditional ceremony and why one puts so much effort into what westerners might mistakenly think of as an afternoon snack. It said, "On time, only once." Meaning that one must put extra effort into making this occasion special because there will never be another like it. That every time you perform the tea ceremony, it is unique and special for different reasons and should be granted the extra attention to detail that your guest will be honored and remember how much you thought of them.

The more I read and the more I learn, the more the concept of beauty in serving makes sense to me. For me, learning to serve as a Geisha is but the greatest challenge I have found thus far. I know it will take many years before my friends will see me as such. I know it will take many more before I am confidant serving a Master as such. I also know that the amount of skills I need to learn before I have earned such a name is far too long to list here. That does not mean that my heart, mind, body and soul does not see it as a worthy goal.

So, on that afternoon lunch date... without even knowing it... I served a man as nothing more than a living piece of art. I was a beautiful woman who helped him relax and made him smile. I was just granting him pleasurable company as we talked and flirted while the sun and wind danced on the surface of the lake.

They say that the first step is the hardest... It was not. Perhaps opening my mind took a while, but the more I read about all I have yet to learn, the more I know that I am no where near my goal. Becoming a Geisha takes years of training... Becoming what I see as a Leather Geisha (more commonly referred to as a Fetish Geisha or the Geisha Model) takes even more.

References:

http://ds-arts.com/GeishaArt/index.html

http://ds-arts.com/RopeArt/mainrope.html

About the Author:

After ten years of marriage, evy knew there was something more out there... As the divorce proceedings came to their conclusion, evy met a Gent, a Master, whom called her "naturally submissive". Shortly there after, evy found Dream Place on Palace Chat where she was evelyn~DP while Tiberious and kat encouraged her to find OPEP. There, she met several members of her local community whom later founded Dominion and OKCKink. Friends and Mentors whom have encouraged her studies, exploration and writing. In the last three years, evy has had poetry published by Sir Ross of leatherweb and has been writing constantly in a variety of forums regarding the lifestyle and her place as a slave.

FUTURE BOOK TITLES FOR THIS *RESOURCE SERIES* OF PUBLICATIONS.

- About Power
- After your Title Year
- Birth and Training of a Leather Master, The
- Book for submissives, The
- Cigar Play
- Coming Out Kinky: The Joys and Sorrows (September)
- Dressed to Kill: fetish dressing in the world of BDSM
- Exploitation vs Ownership - why do they do it?
- Family, Kids, and Kink — Some Challenges
- Generational Differences Affecting BDSMers
- Gorean Relationships
- How to Collect Men
- In Search of Master
- Leather, What is...
- Long-term M/s relationships -- what keeps them together
- Love Issue, The (almost full)
- Medical Play (almost full)
- Multiple Service Relationships
- Objectification
- Physiology - Understanding the human body and how it responds to BDSM play
- Roast Submissive Dinner and other Kinky Recipes
- Rope Bondage and Power Exchange
- SM tools and Power exchange
- Tats, Body Modification, and Scarification
- Transgendered/transsexual
- Vampirism
- What makes a Master?

If you have any interest in writing on any of these topics, please contact: PowerExchangeEditor@Yahoo.com

Articles should be 2,500-3,500 words long; writers' guidelines will be sent upon request.

within REALITY

a lifestyle couple living
life within reality

www.withinreality.com

Made in the USA